www.united-pc-publishing.com

TO Make An Empire

An African New Age Thriller

by

Merc Aurelius

To Make an Empire

"We sleep safely at night because rough men stand ready to visit violence on those who would do us harm."
                    -- Winston Churchill

One

Roy rarely had dreams, and when he did it was a senseless jumble of images which he forgot as soon as he woke up. He also hardly slept in regular seven or eight hour sleep cycles. He usually woke up a few hours after midnight. Rather than lie down doing nothing he would flick on his flashlight and grab any novel he had lying around. There was usually one lying with him in bed. Most times morning would find him with his eyes wide open, reading a book.

And he would be the only one awake amidst dozens at this ungodly hour of the night. He'd actually confirmed that fact one night when, bored, he'd climbed down from his top bunk and exploring the entire boy's hostel.

Not a single person had been awake. Due to the heat and the power outage that struck occasionally, many students had been camped outside. It was two years ago. He'd been in ss1 then, and due to his eccentric nature, he frequently found himself facing the wrath of a senior -- most likely influenced by drugs -- because of some perceived slight.

That night, he'd crept to where a group of them slept, and stood watching them for a while. Completely at his mercy. However, one of them stirred and his heart failed him. He quickly returned to his room and went back to his book.

Now, he was the senior, about to start his school certificate exams. All he really cared about the exams -- the famed WAEC -- was the fact that their end would mark the end of his secondary school. And then he would slowly enter another phase of life that carried with it more responsibilities than that of secondary school student. In the University, he would be responsible for more of his education. He'd heard that he would find freedom when he got admitted into a university. He'd also heard that the government was fighting corruption.

He didn't believe either statement much.

But his beliefs were going to be shaken in a manner he'd never anticipated.

It all started from a meeting of all the exam candidates with the school admin the next morning.

* * *

Roy submitted his answer script and left the hall. A group of his classmates were gathered a few dozen yards away at the football pitch's spectator stands, beaming excitedly about their inevitable success in the latest paper of their West African Senior School Certificate Exams. He went in the opposite direction to the boys' hostel. Other students were still having classes, while most of his classmates were out in the class areas, celebrating their latest landmark. Which meant that no one would be around to disturb his peace.

He removed a novel from under the sheets and lay on his back to read. But his mind was not in it. After a while he gave up and just folded his arms beneath his head and stared at

8

the ceiling. It was not tension from the next exam two days away that nicked at the back of his mind.

Nothing really bothered him about the coming exams. Everything was going according to plan. The school administration, using contributions from students, was greasing the pockets of the government-provided exam invigilators to provide criminally lenient supervisions. That was the result of the meeting that fateful morning a few weeks before the exams.

Except that that was exactly what bothered him. He vividly remembered the way the teachers droned endlessly about the revered WAEC exams throughout his six years in secondary school. And how it was the ultimate screening process for admission into universities. And how it was, to a larger extent, an accurate determinant of future success in life. Like the naive young fool he'd been he'd believed these statements, and had done his best to ensure that his six years at least didn't turn out to be a waste.

So imagine his shock when, a few weeks to the individual registration of the subjects to be written, the SS3 students, along with students from guest schools, were assembled in a confidential location within the school compound, and made to understand that the school admin could help ensure "a smoother exam experience", by "greeting the invigilators in the right way". That *right way* would turn out to come from a projected student contributions of five thousand naira per person.

At that moment, Roy felt like the ground had been pulled out from under him. Here were the same people who'd punished him harshly for offenses as flimsy as not turning in homework, now openly admitting that they had actually been wasting his time all these years. To decieve the public about their incompetence, they would help him obtain impressive results in a standardized test ignorantly revered across Africa. And all it would have required from the very beginning, rather than the weeks of sleepless nights spent preparing for all the previous school termly exams, was a mere five thousand naira and the WAEC registration fees.

He was left quietly seething, and found release for his anger in an altercation with a couple of his classmates that resulted from Roy impulsively making known his feelings of the entire sham. It led him to the realization that , of the country's two hundred million plus population, he was probably the only one who didn't know about the scheme. Which led to him openly declaring that there was no way he could spend a dime on something that turned out to have no real value after all. And that was assuming he could even get his hands on five thousand naira in the first place.

Which in turn led to Roy being frozen out of the teachers' goodwill, so that when photocopied answers to the exams were provided, none found its way to his seat. This was just as well, since he'd become so disillusioned with the entire process that he never opened another notebook after that revelation. His days were

11

now occupied with his novels. At least they were always honest about their lies.

Roy whimsically wondered how his results would turn out at this rate. His father would go wild with rage if he had to resit the exams. He appeared to be the only other person in the country convinced of the validity of the WAEC exams.

In the end he didn't really care. His *father* was no more than a mere benefactor to him, whose only responsibilities were to pay Roy's school fees, fill his stomach, and provide a place to sleep.

Not long after that fateful announcement, he'd begun to entertain impulsive thoughts of just packing up one day and leaving the whole charade of present society. Where he would go, when, and how, were questions he couldn't answer now, but he felt that he would find a way to cross that bridge when the time came.

Roy's thoughts were interrupted when someone entered the room. It was the geography teacher, Mr Addams. He was a reserved young man in his mid-twenties who seemed to Roy like one who had been born with a silver spoon, but had recently come upon evil fortunes to make him ply the school teacher's trade. He hardly spoke, and smiled even less, but he had the deep, calculating eyes most smart people shared. He was the last person Roy expected to be alone in a room with.

"I thought I'd find you here," Mr Addams said.

Roy frowned. That was the oddest thing he expected to hear. "Why were you looking for me?" he said.

"Get up. I want to look at you."

Roy obeyed more out of curiosity than anything else. He sat up to look at the teacher who'd come to intrude in his privacy. And when he did he realized that he had never especially paid Mr Addams any special attention since his appointment in the school at about the time of the WAEC registrations.

He was in his midtwenties -- Roy would say twenty-six -- lean and wiry, with deep intelligent eyes behind clear glasses. He was standing with his hands in his pockets staring emotionlessly at Roy.

Finally, he said, "How are your exams going?"

Roy said nothing at first, searching for any hint of mockery from the teacher. There was none. It turned out to be an innocent and genuine question.

He shrugged in reply. "Well enough," he said, "I guess."

To which Mr Addams arced a brow and smiled. "Are you sure?" he asked.

Roy shrugged again, said nothing more.

"There are eighty-three students registered for this exam," Mr Addams said. "Only five of you failed to pay the agreed five thousand. Out of those five, you're the only one with less than average regular term grades. So why didn't you pay?"

A full minute seemed to pass before Roy spoke. He was wondering if he had an honest answer to the question. In the end he shrugged.

"I don't know," he said. "I guess I just hated the hypocrisy of the whole thing. These are the same teachers that punish you for incomplete notes.

"But that's not the main problem," he continued. "Or the only one. Definitely not every parent is going to support the idea. So who knows the kinds of unscrupulous means their children will have used to acquire the money…."

Roy shook his head. He didn't understand the essence of the questions, and in general Mr Addams' sudden interest in him. For all he knew, the man might be a spy from the school admin, come to indirectly interrogate him. Which was exactly why he continued talking then, and refused to hold anything back.

"It's just so disgusting," he said. "These are the people society has ignorantly entrusted with making sure the younger generation avoid these kinds of corrupt practices. I've heard that it's the same story in most schools -- and even universities too -- across the country. What then is the use of making any effort to try to achieve anything in life, or to make money, when you already have to be five thousand naira rich in secondary school just to scale through. Why not just stick to the place you got the five thousand, and focus on *that* instead of our *schools....*"

Roy's speech hung in the air for a while. He noticed that he was breathing hard, with a lump in his throat, and his eyes stung. Mr Addams, meanwhile, was looking past him, staring into space. Roy realized that he hadn't just answered the payment question, but also the unasked question about his poor grades.

Finally, the teacher said, "You know, there's no teacher in this school that speaks English half as well as you do."

Roy chuckled shyly. "I grew up with foreign novels and comics," he said in reply. Then added, whimsically, "And I'm among the bottom ten in English class."

They both laughed. Right then, Roy felt a spark of something that told him he and this teacher were not much different from each other. Before he could voice the thought, Mr Addams said, "How do you think the problem can be fixed?"

Roy's laughter turned cold. He said, "It can't be fixed. Everyone in the country is involved in the scheme. How can you upset a system that benefits millions of people. You think they'll just sit back and allow things to change? To become more difficult?" He shook his head. "That's how it has always been. That's how it will always be."

"That's a bit pessimistic, don't you think?"

"You don't agree?"

Mr Addams smiled. "No, I don't," he said. "Because that's why I'm here."

Roy frowned. "What do you mean?"

Mr Addams took a deep breath. "Listen very carefully, Roy," he said. He was no longer smiling. "What I'm about to tell you cannot fall on another set of ears. If that happens neither of us is going to like what happens after, you more than me."

Roy said nothing, but it was clear that he understood.

"I work for an organization that wants the same thing you do," Mr Addams said. "We're going to put a stop to all these unethical practices."

Roy looked at him quizzically and laughed drily. "Okay," he said. "Good luck with that. But I'm going to give you a piece of advice, if you want. If this your *organization* pays well, gather up your savings and move to a more *organized* country. You owe it to your children. Because you and your organization are going to fail, simple as that. Corruption and Nigeria are like water and wetness: one is not possible without the other."

Mr Addams chuckled. "You really don't think much of this country, do you?"

Roy shrugged, as if to say, '*Thats just the way it is'*.

"Listen. I know how hard it is to think of this place without all the evil. But trust me, it's going to happen. Much, much sooner than you think. When it happens there are only going to be three kinds of people: those who made it happen, those who watched it happen, and those who'll wonder what happened. Which group do you want to belong?"

Different thoughts were spinning around inside Roy's head. Before he could say anything, Mr Addams pulled out an expensive looking smartphone and handed it to him.

"This is your chance to join the winning team. My superiors need better evidence of these practices than my own words."

Roy took the phone, staring incredulously at Mr Addams. "What do you want me to do?" he said.

Mr Addams smiled. "I'm sure you can think of something."

Two

Up till the next morning, Roy did not know what to think. The phone was a strange foreign model, with active internet connection, but when he checked the network provider, instead of the usual Nigerian networks like MTN or 9mobile, what he saw was *sage.* Otherwise the phone's user interface was what he expected from the latest models of smartphone: sleek of design and vivid of color.

Which brought more questions. This was the most unlikely thing he could have expected in all his life. Even in the books he read, you could expect most of the coming twists. And those were imagined stories. This was real life. And more importantly, this was Nigeria, where dreams… where dreams were never even dreamt in the first place.

He decided to put his misgivings out of his mind and just enjoy the moment. Did he mention that the phone had lightning-fast internet?

* * *

Roy's next exam came three days later. During that time he saw Mr Addams only a couple of times, but the teacher, like all the others, never even acknowledged his existence. Roy obviously couldn't care less.

On the afternoon of the paper, he went inside the hall with the phone. He planned to use it to read his latest novel when he was done answering the questions from whatever lucky points he remembered. Which didn't take up to thirty minutes.

Barely an hour into the exam, the teachers trooped in with the photocopied answers. He had a wry smile as they pointedly walked past his seat. As the students began to take out their phones (unnecessarily, he would say, since they all the answers were already photocopied), Roy did too, and started to subtly take pictures.

He took more than fifty. Because he was bored. Then he got bored of that too, and returned to his books. Another thirty minutes later, he turned in his scantily answered sheet, returned to his room, and wasn't too surprised to find Mr Addams there.

"You have something for me?" the teacher asked.

Roy handed him the phone. He perused the pictures and smiled. Then he winked and left the room without another word. Roy shrugged and hopped onto his bed, and thought himself to sleep.

* * *

Roy thought little of Mr Addams after that. He was only needled because he didn't get to finish the book on the phone. But at seventeen years, he already knew that much about life: it was full of disappointments.

His next paper was another three days away, and it came without incident.

23

He had enough old books and comics to keep him company all the while.

But the day of the exam was followed swiftly by a strange madness.

As usual, the teachers started to spread out answers an hour into the exam. They were only ten minutes into the deed when there was a sudden commotion outside. Several powerful motor engines roared angrily through the school gate and grew louder every second. By the time anyone knew what was going on, three fully loaded camouflaged military trucks had parked outside the hall. The occupants of the vehicles, heavily armed soldiers with masks over their faces -- definitely special forces -- alighted rapidly and trooped into the hall through all five entrances.

It was like a bad dream. All the teachers and students were frozen in place, terrified out of their minds. But things was just getting started.

"EVERYBODY STAND UP AND PUT YOUR HANDS OVER YOUR HEADS."

The order came from the only soldier without a mask. Roy guessed he was the leader.

The order was obeyed without a second's delay. Two men in black suits, who'd also entered with the soldiers, went up to the exam supervisor's table and showed their badges.

"Miss Olu-oti?" one of them said to the woman, who replied with a terrified whimper. "You're under arrest for betraying the trust of the federal government by being an accomplice to examination malpractice…"

By then, the soldiers had rapidly combed through the hall with plastic bags, seizing every illegal item they could find. Which was all of it, since nobody could muster the nerve to try to hide anything.

When they were done, the commanding soldier, along with three more, went up to the men in suits.

"Take this thing out of my sight," one Suit said, and two soldiers promptly grabbed the woman, clapped handcuffs on her hands, and marched her out of the hall.

The same Suit announced, to everyone in the hall, "Pack your bags and go home. Come back next year when you're well prepared." Then they left.

Five minutes later, there was no sign that any such incident had occurred, except for the stunned students and teachers, and the tension in the room so thick you could cut it with a knife.

Only one student didn't share their bewilderment.

Roy was feeling something different. He sat down and stared in a trance. Butterflies swarmed in his stomach. He really couldn't believe it. It was all so unreal. But one thing was for sure: Mr Addams had been telling the truth after all.

Three

The evening after the stunning incident, the school proactively called an assembly of the WAEC candidates. They explained that they were working to resolve the strange issue, and had come to a decision to give the students a short break while they sorted things out.

The teachers did their best to regard the matter as lightly as they dared. They didn't want to admit what they knew was likely to result from the morning's fiasco, and were hoping that the mass of teenagers would be too naive and airheaded to understand.

The truth was, most of the students were just excited about having to get a break from the incredibly structural school system. Outside these prison walls, they all lived different and more exciting lives.

One of the main source of excitement was that the Marvel Studios' Black Panther movie had been released two months ago, while they were still in school. The sudden break would give all of them a chance to see it in cinemas. Roy would get a chance to see it too, since there was now a cinema back home in Lokoja. Actually, the FNX mega mall (pronounced "finix", like the magical bird) that had opened less than a year ago, had a theatre where blockbuster movies were shown.

But Roy didn't care about cartoons right now. Reality had just gotten interesting. Whether he liked it or not he was partially responsible for having a woman-- a mother -- arrested. The exam didn't even seem as serious compared to that.

When the group dispersed, he searched all over the school for Mr Addams but found no sign of him. He realized that he hadn't even seen the man since he returned the phone.

It didn't take long for Roy to realize that he was never going to see Mr Addams -- if that was really his name -- ever again. Clearly the man's work here was done. So he bottled his disappointment and packed his bags. When he was done, he went to his housemaster to place a call home. To break a news that would have already reached home via email and text message from the school.

As usual there was no sentiment between father and son, only empty pleasantries and an offhand wish for a safe trip home. The housemaster would drive him to the park the next morning.

Roy's past experiences had developed in him an unreasonable phobia of going home. His rational mind knew there was nothing to fear. Whenever he was actually home, he hardly ever saw his father, who left for work before dawn and returned after dusk. But it didn't stop the little boy in him from plaguing him with anxiety.

That night, he couldn't sleep. And he couldn't focus enough to read either. He just snapped his eyes shut and suffered in silence.

He was feeling better the next day and managed to sleep on the four hour trip back home. Even though he was crushed between four people at the back of a station wagon. He arrived home cramped and sore by early noon. His father would still be another hour or so before coming home for his ritual of homemade lunch.

Roy knocked on the gate, and after waiting ten minutes, he realized no one was home. The maid was probably at the market, so, rather than wait under the scalding Lokoja sun, he skipped over the fence and opened the gate from the inside. The maid and his father would return none the wiser, and he could remain undisturbed at least till nightfall.

He settled into his familiar musty room, with a dusty floor that would soon be covered with the worn rags that passed for his clothes. Snacking on some appetizers obtained at the only stop on the journey here, he took up one of the books he left behind, snuggled in his bare mattress, and burned away the time.

Later that evening, he learnt from the maid that his father was away on a business trip. Roy knew that these trips could last anything from a day to more than a week, so he didn't really get his hopes up. But at least some of the tension left him.

* * *

His father returned the next evening. Due to Roy's isolated lifestyle, his old man always got the impression that he was asleep whenever he returned for lunch, or in the evenings after closing up for the day. And since his father usually spent his weekends at his hometown, their paths hardly ever crossed. Unless his father needed some manual labor. And even then, he considered Roy too weak and airheaded to do any serious work.

The zombie-like maid came to inform him of his father's arrival. Roy gave the man enough time to clean up and start eating before going to place a formal greeting. Because then his scathing tongue would be too occupied with food to toss any insults Roy's way.

The evening news was on, and Roy saw a not-so-surprising headline boldly displayed at the bottom of the screen, declaring that the 2018/19 Waec exams had been cancelled.

The gist of the news explained that the decision had been made by the federal government, following investigations by the latest federal agency, established only a year ago: the National Investigations Council. The operation was carried out in more than two hundred private and public secondary schools nationwide, on charges of examination malpractice. The anchor added that despite mass public outcry, there was no hope that the decision would be reversed, and it was only the first step in finally curing the country of the chronic crime and corruption that had plagued it for decades.

Roy tuned out the rest of the broadcast and observed his father's reaction. He wouldn't be surprised if the man was scrutinizing the report for something to blame him for. And as if upset that he found no part of

it to pin on Roy, his only reply to
his greeting was a sour grumble.

Roy thought nothing of it and
returned to his room with his dinner.
He was overcome by a strange
euphoria, and hummed a tune as he
juggled between reading and eating.

He didn't know it yet, but things
were just going to get better.
Starting with Mr Addams coming to
take him away.

Four

The fateful day began like any other.

His father had left for work by the time Roy got out for breakfast. He returned to his room with his food and gobbled it down before going back to his books. He usually lost track of time when reading, and by ten a.m, the power came, but since he had no phone or any other electronic device, he was unmoved. While the maid would surely be glued to her mindless telenovelas in the living room.

As usual, his father came home from lunch at half past one, but what was most unusual was that he had sent for Roy after another half hour of his arrival. And when he went to meet him, who else would he find in the living room with his father but Mr Addams?

"Good afternoon," he said to them in turn.

"Roy," his father said, "this is Mr Kunle. He's a representative of..?"

he glanced at the man Roy knew as Mr Addams inquisitively.

"Prodigy Foundation," Mr Addams -- or Kunle -- said.

"Yes, yes," his father said, and continued. "It's a special school in Abuja that caters specifically to your type of learning disabilities. They're making rounds across the country, because of this strange WAEC incident, and they're granting scholarships to try to reduce the number of idle kids that will surely fill the streets now…." He handed Roy a card which turned out to be the school's brochure. Roy thought it looked convincing.

"You're lucky," his father added. "Or maybe I am. At least God is not going to let you waste away your life eating and sleeping."

The comment was water off a duck's back. Roy was busy watching Mr Addams. Neither of them gave any hint they knew each other, the man more so. Roy didn't find it hard to believe that this was a Mr Kunle from a certain special school, though he knew better. He knew that this man could claim to be anything, and no one would have any trouble believing it.

And he also knew that the identity wasn't wholly false. It could be true that the man had come to take Roy to a certain special school. What kind however, was left to his own imagination. And it really wasn't hard to imagine, though he would wait to find out whether he was right.

In the end Roy decided not to bother himself with the uncertain future. What would come would come. There was no use worrying himself sick about it.

His father was talking. "I already told him you'll be interested," he said. "So get your things together. He'll come for you tomorrow morning."

Roy nodded, and, seeing that the discussion was over, returned to his room. He was overwhelmed with mixed feelings. On the one hand he was disgusted that his father had already made the decision for him, completely oblivious of what he was getting Roy into. And on the other, he realized that this was exactly what he'd been waiting for. The bridge he would cross had come much sooner and much more straightforward than he'd expected.

He had no idea what was going to happen next, once he was alone with the man who was both Mr Addams and Mr Kunle. But, like all worthy things in life, he knew it would be worth the wait.

He wasn't disappointed.

* * *

He came by ten a.m. Roy had packed only a bag with his few usable clothes. More than half of the space was occupied by all his novels and comics. Mr Addams had come in a glossy black car with tinted windows, so Roy could see his reflection clearly.

Roy hardly ever used a mirror. Usually, it took a second look for him to recognize himself in photographs -- whenever he bothered to take any. But this time, something made him pause and stare at his image.

He was lean and pale, not surprising, due to his isolated lifestyle, and about average height. Years of staring at nothing but books had given him dark, serious eyes. And his detachment from society fixed a perpetual frown on his face.

Roy took one last look and then got in the back seat. Somehow, he knew he would never see that particular face again.

Mr Addams got in beside him. And then the driver started the car and cruised away.

Roy was surprised to see that the driver was white, but he said nothing, and instead resumed the rereading of one of his older books. About ten minutes in, he noticed that Mr Addams was staring at him.

"What?" he said.

Mr Addams tilted his head in amusement. "I have to say that you're taking all this a bit too calmly," he said. "Any normal person would have more than a few questions."

Roy closed the book. "So maybe I'm not normal."

"Yeah. No shit."

"Well, actually, I'm curious about a couple of things. I was only waiting for you to ask first. Because then it'll be less likely that you'll give me false answers."

Mr Addams could not hide his elation. He said, "Reverse psychology. I knew there was no mistake about you."

Roy looked curiosly at him and said, "Are you ready?"

"Fire away."

"Alright. So, the first question -- and I think it's the most important one. Who are you, really?"

The man with the false names smiled. "You know," he said, "that other than outright lying I can give you half-truths that wouldn't be any better."

"I'm going to hope that you won't," Roy said. "Wherever it is you're taking me, I'll be very grateful for anything that would make me avoid any ignorant mistakes. Because I feel like even right now I'm already being evaluated."

"*Evaluated,*" Mr Addams repeated with a smile. "You know all the right terms…" He paused at that for a moment, his mind distant. Then he said, "Okay, about your question. Were you asking about me personally, or the organization I work for."

"Both."

"Okay then, let's start with me. I know you're wondering about my name, and you're both right and wrong in thinking that my name isn't really

Addams. Because it is, and it isn't. I'll explain. But I hope you can take it…

"You see, me, you, everybody," he continued, "we can be whatever we want to be, whenever we want. But only particularly advanced minds know how.

"Mr Addams was a secondary school geography teacher, and for as long as was necessary, I *was* him. But his job is done, and now I'm back to my default self. Which is whoever I want to be, depending on…" He paused and laughed briefly. "Actually," he continued, "it depends on my mood, which is a product of my ego, my lower self. And at the academy we are taught that the measure of success in our profession rests solely on the ability to detach from the ego. Always easier said than done.

"But I was born Ahmad," he added, "if you still want to know. No *Mister* attached."

Roy silently absorbed the information. None of what the man --

named Ahmad from birth -- said was strange to him. He was conversant with the subject of multiple personalities from his long history of fictional stories. But they always treated the condition like it was a neurotic illness. Yet here was someone who willingly employed it, and it wasn't odd to think that Roy was going to be taught to do so as well.

"Okay," he said, "second question. What did you really need me for? You already knew about the school's exam traditions. You could have ended the whole thing right from the beginning. So why did you come to me?"

"Because my assignment wasn't to stop anything," Ahmad replied.

"What was it, then?"

Ahmad paused briefly, then said, "To recruit you."

For some reason the statement hit like a battering ram.

Recruit him? But why? He was nothing. He knew less than nothing, and could do even less than that. He'd never achieved anything for anyone to take such an interest in him.

He didn't hide his misgivings. "I don't understand," he said. "I'm nothing. I don't see what would make you go through all that trouble. There are millions of better candidates for whatever it is you need me for. You should have asked my father. He'll convince you."

Ahmad laughed at that. He said, "That realization alone, of the reality of your own insignificance and worthlessness, is enough to serve our purpose. Because you weren't chosen for what you are, but what you can become, under the proper guidance."

Roy fell back in his seat and quietly blew out his cheeks. He wanted to say something, but for a long time his mind was blank.

Finally, he said, "One more thing. Actually it's an extension of the first. You forgot to tell me about your organization."

"It'll be much more fun if you find that out yourself," Ahmad said with a smile.

The car cut into a remote field, in the middle of which sat a black helicopter, it's rotors cycling lazily. Roy stared.

"Let's go figure it out," Ahmad said, and together they got out of the car.

Five

Moving thousands of feet above the ground was a truly amazing experience, but like with all the other experiences in his life, Roy tempered his excitement with the fact that, though slim, there was a chance of a malfunction and then the helicopter would plunge them down to their doom.

At first he gazed outside the window at the scenery of buildings and streets below, but it soon got boring. He was terrible at even the local geography, so after a while everything below looked the same. But not for long. Soon, the only thing below was dense forest, and as the helicopter started to slow, he wondered if that was the final destination.

It would be terribly disappointing, but what exactly had he been expecting. He closed his eyes and withdrew into himself, not sleeping but not exactly awake either. He felt them descend gradually, and took another look outside. His lips curved into a curious smile.

They were heading for a small clearing in the middle of the woods, where about seven helicopters were already parked. Some of them were empty, but from a couple of others he could see the passengers drop and make their way to a small line of military trucks -- humvees. The passengers were a pair, an adult and a kid about his age. It appeared that he wasn't the only recruit in the program.

Soon he and Ahmad were making their way to their own truck. He breathed in the smell of damp earth as they walked, and then lost himself behind the roar of the truck as they drove through a trail in the forest that had been completely invisible from above.

The truck stopped at the edge of a spacious courtyard, bounded by a cluster of huts separated into two blocks. The other kids were sitting in small groups at picnic tables set to one side of the yard. There were about two dozen tables, which meant enough empty space for a loner to occupy. Their bags were with them, and Roy noticed that, like him, they'd all packed light. He also noticed that the adults were absent.

He turned to Ahmad. "What now?"

"Now, you wait here," Ahmad replied. "Dr Fash will address you all shortly."

Roy frowned. "Dr Who?"

Ahmad laughed at his own joke. "Don't worry," he said. "Just a silly joke."

Roy shrugged with disinterest. He grabbed his bag and book and got out of the truck, which then turned and shot back down the trail. He chose a table furthest from the nearest group and resumed his book, paying no mind to the inquisitive stares shot in his direction.

* * *

Meanwhile, a few hundred yards away, a group of people were in a control room, watching a live video feed of the kids in the yard. They included all twenty-seven handlers who'd been tasked with recruiting the kids, the camp's instructors and auxiliary staff like medics and the psychologist, and finally the director herself. Together they comprised of the brightest minds specially cropped from the country's originally ineffective law enforcement community. The instructors and auxiliary staff had all received extensive training from foreign nations light-years ahead of Nigeria in special operations. Countries that traced their experience back to the Second World War.

The entire operation was a secret branch of the NIC, tasked with recruiting and training young soldiers who would be genuine assets in the organization's battle against the epidemic of corruption in the country.

The camp's existence was known to only three other people in the world outside of the room. They were the Grand Commander of the Federation -- the president himself, the director of the NIC, and his deputy.

There was also one other person, known only to the director of the secret group. Even in that limited circle, he would never be associated with the program, even though he was the brains behind the entire thing.

Right now, the group in the control room were making individual assessments of the kids. But there was no need, really. With the kind of training regimen they had planned, anyone who could tie their shoelaces and remember their own names could be made to serve their purpose.

"All right everyone," the director said, "let's go and give our new operatives a big welcome."

* * *

About thirty minutes after Roy had arrived, there was a sudden cacophony of multiple engines that caused all conversation to cease. He closed his book with a mild annoyance as the trucks appeared. He'd just gotten to the story's climax.

There were two dozen trucks in all. The passengers all flushed out en masse, including the drivers, so there was soon a large crowd more than fifty adults in the middle of the courtyard, all buzzing with a vibrant energy.

The leader of the group was unmistakable. She was a five foot tall boxy woman with a wizened face. The whole crowd seemed to form around her. When she spoke, it was fluent and without any accent, local or foreign. She would be perfectly at home anywhere as a wealthy noblewoman, with her aristocratic gravitas.

Roy wouldn't admit it, but he liked her already. He knew she bore no illusions about the world. And he -- along with all the other kids --

would learn that this was true for all personnel at the camp.

"Hello, everyone," she said. "I am Dr Fashola…" she glanced behind her and added, "though some people call me Dr Fash behind my back."

This drew sheepish looks from the crowd behind her, and giggles from the kids.

"Anyway," she continued, "I know most of you are smart enough to have at least an idea of why you're here. If not, you wouldn't be here in the first place."

Roy noticed the other kids beaming. He felt the same flutter they were feeling from the complement, but he forced himself to remain composed. This place might be different, but the words of adults carried little weight with him. They were all a bunch of hypocrites.

As if in answer to his thoughts, Dr Fash continued, saying, "I know some of you may not trust me. Or any of us, in fact. Because the adults in your lives have not given you the best impression. Including your parents, unfortunately. Those of you that still do have parents, that is. But perhaps the first thing you'll learn here is that just because someone messed something up, doesn't mean it has to stay that way…."

She paused, and her bearing became even more serious. "Which brings us to why you're here," she said. "Supposing I asked you to list all the countries you would have preferred to be born in, what number would Nigeria come?"

A loud, sneering laughter burst from the kids. But Dr Fash wasn't smiling. In turn, the laughter was quickly hushed.

"You're right to laugh," she said. "Your country is a joke. Not just here at home, but all over the planet. Now I ask: how much longer does it have to be like that?"

The kids looked sombre. No one said a word.

She continued. "The officials we've entrusted with our lives have made a real mess of things. They blame and pick on you, the younger generation, while masking their greed and insecurities with political lip-service. But I'll tell you now: you people are the only solution, and they are the problem."

Roy looked away from her, but no one used eyes to hear. He hated her words, because they were true. And spoken like that gave him hope. Hope that he did not want. He hated everyone. He hated this damned country. He hated the world. And that was all he was. If things could change, what then would become of him?

Again, she answered his thoughts. "Yes, you may never have heard this before, but you are the only ones that can right our wrongs. A few of us oldies have come to this realization, but all we can do is guide you. We can only lead you to the cliff. You are the ones who would have to take that leap of faith…."

As she spoke, a group of the younger members of her posse, Ahmad included, went to the kids. They were carrying thin black folders. Roy guessed that the others were also handlers as Ahmad placed the folder on the table before him, and returned. The twenty-six others did the same thing.

On the cover of the folder was a crest of the NIC, an airborne eagle carrying a large golden orb in its talons. But closer inspection revealed that this one was different. The bird's feathers were curved like fangs, so that it looked rather like a Phoenix than an eagle; and unlike the original, this one bore no initials. And it was in black and white.

It said that this was the emblem of the NIC Secret Service.

"Open it," she said.

Roy's hands trembled as he did. He stared.

Across the first page was stamped, in bold red letters, the word

CLASSIFIED. The next page was like a CV. It had his passport on one corner, with columns for his personal details, a short biography, and finally, covering the lower half of the page, was a newspaper clipping with the same headline as the news broadcast a couple of nights ago. He looked with shock down the rows of picnic tables at the other kids. They were doing the same thing.

"That was your first assignment. And you all did remarkably. In only one day the twenty-seven of you dealt a sizeable blow to the enemy. But examination malpractice is just one tip of a mountain-sized iceberg. We all have a lot of work to do to cure this country of corruption. But it can be done, one successful assignment at a time.

"You will all be given a three-week assessment period wherein you will learn about the requirements of this path we are asking you to take." She paused and looked them all round, and added, "I should add beforehand the saying: to make an omelette, you first have to break eggs.

"To make good soldiers, good professionals, we are going to have to break the amateur within you." She smiled. "Good luck soldiers, and God be with you."

<u>Six</u>

The assessment process began the very
next morning, at three a.m exactly.
After the previous day's assembly,
they'd all been given, along with the
necessary gear for their first two
weeks in the camp, a briefing of
their daily routine. So no one was
surprised when the housemasters, two
each for the boys and girls, arose
them with shrill whistling in the
dead of night.

It didn't mean they were all
prepared, however. More than half of
them, Roy included, were still
snuggling in their cots even through
the piercing noise. The housemasters,
who also doubled as their fitness
instructors, solved that problem with
bucketfuls of freezing water.

By half past three, they were all on
track, in their sweatsuits and
trainers, for a light three mile jog.
Dawn had just broken when they
returned to their dormitories, all
drenched in sweat and panting hard.
The instructors, who'd jogged along
with them all the three miles, were

barely flushed. What followed was an hour of a gruelling series of calisthenic exercises in the courtyard that left the kids too sore to walk to their rooms. Most of them did not bother to shower after, until they'd recovered what sleep they'd lost.

But breakfast was ready at nine, only half an hour after the workout. And since they would rather be sleepless than hungry, they had to drag themselves out of bed to the showers, and then to the picnic tables. They were at the brink of despair when they found that breakfast consisted only of fruit salad with chicken and yogurt. Where was the bread? The yams? The foods that would recover all the energy they'd lost that morning?

The housemasters explained that those foods were harder to digest, and, even though they were energy giving carbohydrates, drained a person throughout the day after only an hour or two of high energy. And warriors -- for they were all warriors in

training -- had to be at their peak
at every moment.

They were allowed second rounds
though, and every single one of them
accepted the offer eagerly.

They were then left to themselves
until ten o'clock. They were allowed
to explore the dorm areas, except
their opposite genders' rooms, and
they spent most of that time in the
courtyard, getting more acquainted
with each other, sharing as much of
their personal histories as each
dared. They all admitted that they
actually felt pretty good after the
exercise and ruminant breakfast.

Roy, meanwhile, got more acquainted
with his books. Even though he and
the others all had one thing in
common -- each of them sharing the
same status as social outcasts in the
outside world in varying degrees --
most of them were adjusted enough to
be able to hold conversations with
strangers. He wasn't that lucky. He
was aware that in here they would
drill it out of him. But he would

enjoy his awkwardness while it
lasted.

At half past ten everyday, they were
herded out to an auditorium where
they were lectured on a variety of
subjects.

They were taught the histories of the
battles of the warriors of light
against the always overwhelming
forces of darkness. The battles of
freedom and liberty, against slavery
and subjugation. They learnt of the
Battle of Thermopylae, where only
three hundred Spartan warriors --
with a few thousand auxiliary troops
from neighboring states -- stood
against the Persian army led by king
Xerxes, whose men were in the
millions.

And they learnt of the Spartan King's
iconic phrase when asked by the enemy
to lay down their arms: "Come and get
them," King Leonidas had quipped.

They learnt how the world's foremost
nation on human freedom and liberty,
the United States of America, gained
their independence from the British

in the famed American Revolution. And also how a great American fought his brothers for the emancipation of black slaves in the American Civil War.

Those were the foremost of their lessons, but not the last. Along with geography, the social and pure sciences and mathematics, they also learnt what it meant to be warriors and soldiers, individuals and team players. They were taught loyalty to their values and intuition. They were taught that discipline was the only way to true freedom, with the iconic statement : "A man is free to the level of his own self mastery. And those who fail to govern themselves will always be doomed to find masters to govern them."

* * *

By the end of the the three weeks, the kids had been sufficiently transformed both physically and mentally, so that no one outside of the camp could ever mistake them for who the once were. Physically they walked erect, not with the slight weak stoop most regular people moved with. They no longer needed the housemasters to wake them up for the three mile run. Their eyes snapped open at about three a.m exactly. And the run no longer terrified them, rather they relished it. They became agile, always resonating vibrant energy from their intense exercises and healthy diet.

Six months of real labour would follow this assessment period. But they knew they would be ready for whatever the camp instructors could cook up. Just as each one of them knew they would be selected. They all had that unshakable faith in themselves.

They had developed the mind and body of regular warriors. The next six months would take their training to another level, to make them truly special warriors.

On the evening of the twenty-first day, the entire camp gathered, just like on their very first day here, for a quiet enlistment ceremony. A raging bonfire added to the surrealism of the event.

The recruits were dressed in finely cut suits for the boys and elegant dresses for the girls. This was their rite of passage. They stood in formation as they prepared to be officially drafted into the NIC Secret Service. They would become officers of a flawed federation, but one which could become prosperous if steered in the right direction. They would work in the shadows, unlike regular law enforcement, doing the dirty work necessary to create that reality. It would be difficult, but they had been conditioned to despise ease. They would have it no other way.

After a brief address by Dr Fash in her usual genial manner, they lifted up their right hands to take the Special Forces warrior oath. After being made to understand exactly what it entailed.

It went thus:

"I am a Special Forces soldier. A professional! I will do all that my nation requires of me.

I am a volunteer, knowing well the hazards of my profession.

Realizing that I am the first of a new legacy, I pledge to uphold the honor and integrity of all I am – in all I do.

I am a professional warrior. I will teach and fight wherever my nation requires. I will strive always, to excel in every art and artifice of my trade.

I know that I will be called upon to perform tasks in isolation, far from familiar faces and voices, with the help and guidance of my God.

I will keep my mind and body clean, alert and strong, for this is my debt to those who depend upon me.

I will not fail those with whom I serve. I will not bring shame upon myself or the forces.

I will maintain myself, my arms, and my equipment in an immaculate state as befits a Special Forces soldier, and a warrior.

I will never surrender though I be the last. If I am taken, I pray that I may have the strength to spit upon my enemy.

My goal is to succeed in any mission - and live to succeed again.

I am a member of my nation's chosen soldiery. God grant that I may not be found wanting, that I will not fail this sacred trust."

After that there was a round of applause and cheers from the camp staff, before the new soldiers had their agency pins pinned on their chests. Pins that could not burst the steely pride swelling within them.

Seven

They were to undergo a camp-
prescribed basic training for another
six months. Within the first few
weeks of that time, the new agents
realized that the initial three week
assessment period had been meant to
prepare them for the hell of these
six months, which was designed to
push them past the the threshold of
human physical and mental endurance.

The morning run was doubled to six
miles, and they ran the course with
sixty pounds worth of weights
specially designed for their limbs
and torso. For the first week the
kids could barely walk. But no one
asked for the weights to be taken
off. They knew it would only be a
matter of time before their bodies
adapted. If only they refused to
quit.

It took two weeks for them to start
to jog, a few meters at a time.
Another two weeks later, they covered
the six miles at a steady jog for the
first time.

They spent two months before they could move with the weights as if they weren't there. To prevent overly developed muscles from routinely carrying twice their bodyweight for hours at a time, they were treated with acupuncture needles, as well as some special injections to boost physical endurance by reducing muscle fatigue.

A whole three months was spent on this physical therapy alone. Their exercises in that time -- done with the weights, mind you -- consisted largely of balance, coordination, and agility drills. By the time the weights were finally taken of, their muscles felt like they were carved from rock.

Running without the weights, they could clock up to forty miles per hour for more than a mile before starting to feel the first signs of fatigue. That made them faster than any recorded human in history.

It would only get better.

Combat training followed soon after. They learnt about the human body, about the numerous clusters of nerves that could paralyze, knock unconscious, or kill with varying levels of pressure. They were routinely pitted to spar against multiple opponents at a time, who were under instructions not to hold back. And the kids almost always came out on top.

They were also warned that fighting should be a last resort, only when it couldn't be avoided, as, the instructors explained, the best fights were won without fighting in the first place. For that they were taught another skill at the other end of the human fight or flight response to threats: they learnt how to run away.

Freerunning, or parkour, involved navigating an urban environment like it was one giant obstacle course. A proficient parkourist was almost impossible to capture or outrun, as even storey buildings were scaled as easily as if they were ten foot walls.

All the while, they were taught to master the three basic Nigerian languages. In those six months, the new agents were trained to become more than mere soldiers. They were groomed into forces of nature. Supersoldiers, if you prefer, whose physical and mental capabilities would pale even that of the ancient Spartans.

The time flew like the wind. The agents were surprised to find out one day that their basic training was over. They would all be returning home the next day.

Once again the camp gathered at the courtyard. The new agents were made to understand their status and purpose as the secret guardians of the nation.

"Most law enforcement -- in better countries," Dr Fash explained, "protect the cultures and identities of the societies they are charged to defend. But the Nigerian culture has been corrupted by tribalism and vested interests. The citizens have identified with this corruption to the extent that it has become their accepted way of life. And they will fight to keep it that way.

"The magnitude of the problem is enough to cause anyone who dreams of a better world to despair. But still, here we are…."

She continued, stating that most wars had been fought -- and won -- from what first appeared to be a crippling disadvantage. The famed battle of Thermopylae, for instance. A handful of warriors against an army that outnumbered them three thousand to one. Sure, all three hundred Spartans lost their lives in the end, but their brave sacrifice rallied the rest of Greece together and the Persian threat was finally overcome.

But it had to start from the sacrifice from a few people's indomitable desire to do what was right, despite the odds.

The new agents, unlike those three hundred, had a much better advantage over the enemy. Aside from their superior training, they had the element of surprise, in that the enemy didn't know they were coming. The battles would also not be fought in an open field where numbers mattered. They would be fought in the shadows.

The agents would be ghosts. The enemy would never see them coming. That was why they were going to win. One successful assignment at a time.

The last thing they learnt, and which threatened to sour their entire experience before leaving the camp, was that they would not just be idling at home with unlimited amounts of leisure time and resources. The school session would be resuming in a month. There would be a mandatory four week extension period, monitored by the board of education along with NIC agents, for all the schools to create a crash revision course to better prepare the students for the exams, which will then be completely restarted, all questions reset.

After Dr Fash's speech, the agents were each issued a briefcase

71

containing a laptop computer, a satellite smartphone, and field communication devices -- in the form of tiny earpieces with nearly unlimited range. Along with ATM cards with access to a net account. All their gadgets were connected to the agency's unique server, *sage,* which was provided by their own personal satellite.

Together with the training, personnel, and the Research and Development department that provided field equipment, the agency's budget was three quarters that of the entire nation's annual allocation.

And it was all thanks to one man.

* * *

After the kids' sending off, Dr Fash got on phone to inform that man of the success of the operation. The country now had twenty-seven formidable soldiers to fight for her.

"You're sure they're ready?" he asked. "No complications?"

"How could there be?" she said jokingly. "You were the one who planned it, weren't you."

"I'm not above mistakes, Fash," he said.

"Trust me, they're ready."

"We'll see," he said, and hung up.

Fash set the phone aside, and prepared to sleep for the first time in six months. It had not been an easy ride at all. There had always been the fear that something would go wrong. These were just teenagers after all.

Most of their training had been experimental, and there was always the fear that they could all go into cardiac arrest at any time due to the incredible strain being placed on their minds and bodies. Also, the medications consistently administered to the kids during the training weren't simply steroids. They were a crude attempt to create a super-soldier serum, designed to improve strength, endurance and physical and mental stamina over extended periods of time. And it could have backfired any number of ways. It could still produce undesirable side effects in the future. For now though, she was going to keep her fingers crossed.

Fash would never have agreed to this whole operation if it was anyone other than Haruna Abdul who'd suggested it.

The world believed Aliko Dangote to be the wealthiest black man on the planet. But that was because they were comparing his wealth to that of other individuals. Had they been seeking someone whose wealth could be compared against nations, then perhaps Abdul might have revealed his standing. Or he might not, seeing as he was most averse to the public limelight.

The man was wealthier than most prosperous nations on the African continent, with more than a few leading organizations in every field of industry. He was also unarguably the smartest man she'd ever met, able

74

in an instant to procure solutions to problems he'd never encountered before. And a very small number of people knew him, because a crippling social anxiety was one of his many quirks. They were old schoolmates, him and Fash, which was why she knew.

That was also why she took a second look when he presented her with this initiative. His solution to Nigeria's corruption and mediocrity. At first glance, it was blatantly illegal, sure to bring the wrath of any democracy, local or foreign. But on the other hand, it was very likely to work.

Most people involved in the NIC Secret Service believed that it was part of the federal government program. But they were wrong. The entire country would be crippled if it actually had to finance the agency's covert operations branch for even a month.

Fash suspected that the official NIC itself was also his idea, a front to hide his main agenda. Because it was not just one West African country he

planned to fix. The same problems
plagued all world Nations in
different degrees. And his goal was
to fix it all.

Eight

Roy's return home was the same as how he left. A helicopter from the camp, to the field, and then a three hour drive to the front gate. And like before, Ahmad was with him.

"Take care of yourself," his handler said when it came time to part. "We're going green in a week. And remember, always keep a low profile. No extravagant stuff. No showing off."

Roy nodded. Going green meant working on a new assignment. He couldn't wait. They shook hands, and he got out of the car with his briefcase. Before the car drove away, he glanced at his reflection on the window and smiled.

He was still lean, but athletic now, rather than emaciated. There were subtler changes, invisible to the untrained eye, which was ninety-nine percent of Nigerians. The most prominent one was the confident twinkle in his eyes that made him appear to be laughing inside at

everything he looked at. Most times
he was.

For a while Roy stood in the sun
alone, doing and thinking of nothing,
simply breathing and being. Finally,
he knocked on the gate. He couldn't
get the smile off his face. Soon,
there was a shuffle of footsteps and
then the gate's peephole was opened
and a pair of eyes filled the space.

"Yes?" the maid -- no, her name was
Glory -- eyed him once and said. "Who
are you looking for?"

Roy's reply was a ludicrous smile.
She was about to speak again when
recognition dawned on her. She
gasped.

Immediately, she opened the gate,
staring at him like she was seeing a
ghost. Roy gave her a courteous nod
and walked past her into the
compound. He went around the back to
his room, and cringed when he opened
the door.

Nothing had actually changed. The
floor was still littered and dusty,

and the place smelled like an abandoned wine cellar. It was just that he was a different person now. It wouldn't do to have his quarters in such condition. He only took off his shirt before setting about making the place liveable.

He cleared out all his worn clothes -- which turned out to be *all* his clothes -- as well as any other useless items. In the end all that survived his clear out were the bare mattress and the room's four dimensions. He swept and mopped the floor, before wearing his shirt and leaving the house.

He returned half an hour later with a boxload of new clothes and sheets for his bed. After making the bed, he folded the clothes neatly in a box, then left again to get something to eat. When he returned home later that evening, he learnt that his dad was away on another trip, and had packed enough clothes for a week.

Roy spent the rest of the evening reading on his phone. But by midnight, that particular activity that he'd enjoyed for the better part of his conscious life had become dull and monotonous. He just couldn't stand being stagnant anymore. So he called Ahmad.

"Hey," Ahmad said. "Trouble sleeping?"

"Kind of," Roy replied. "Listen, I was wondering…. About the next op. What's it about? Why the one week delay?"

Ahmad chuckled. He didn't blame the kid for his eagerness. Once you became a part of the shadow world, your old world lost its allure. Which would hit an isolationist like Roy twice as hard. But he still had to learn that patience was a major part of their craft.

"We're going after the drug trade," Ahmad explained. "We're trying to gather up enough intel before we move."

Roy said nothing. He was thinking.

"Upstairs thinks there's no more than a dozen big dogs responsible for smuggling it into the country. They're the real targets; the kingpins. Our job is to identify them and get enough evidence for the NIC guys to legally put them behind bars."

He continued. "There's a complex pyramid of about five levels involved in the drug trade. The kingpins are at the top, and the network is filtered and branched out, right down to the regular pushers on the streets. The plan is to get the right street-level pusher that can lead us to any one of these kingpins. If not," he added, "we can waste valuable time barking up the wrong tree."

Roy was still silent. There were a couple of holes in Ahmad's plan, but he couldn't put his mind on it. Until….

"Wait a minute," he said sharply. Then, much more calmly, "You really believe we need a week for all that?

We're not even starting the fun stuff till then?"

"You have a better plan?"

"Actually, I do. And it shouldn't take up to half of one week to find your kingpins."

Ahmad chuckled. "Hold on a minute. Before you tell me your great *plan*," he said, a mild sarcasm in his adjective. "The entire crew is working this same op throughout the country. All twenty-seven of us. Our movements have to be in sync."

"That's easy," Roy said. "Everyone will just follow my plan."

Ahmad laughed again. "Alright Sherlock, let's hear it."

"Okay, it's like this. You said any one of these street pushers is a part of this pyramid, right?"

"Yes."

"Well then, why don't we just grab one and shake him up till he reveals *his* source. And then we grab *that* guy, and keep working like that till we get to the top. Simple as that. In fact, we don't need to get the kingpins themselves. Anyone two levels above the streets should have enough material for the NIC to make their arrests."

It was Ahmad's turn to be silent. He was working up a counter to that plan. It just sounded too easy to work.

Finally, he said, "There's too much risk involved, Roy. Any hint the network is being attacked and the top guys can just vanish. They have enough money to live without want in any foreign country for the rest of their lives."

"Only if we get sloppy," Roy said. "Which we won't. Think about it. These guys have successfully run their operations without any hitch for at least a decade. They've obviously grown arrogant and complacent. They'll never suspect a thing. They'll be communicating with their lawyers behind bars before they even know what hit them."

Ahmad didn't even have to think it through. There was no arguing with the kid's logic. "I'll send you an address," he said, conceding. "Meet me there in the morning."

"How about right now?"

"Well, unlike you, Batman, I actually have to sleep."

Roy chuckled. "Seven, then," he said, and hung up.

Nine

At 3 a.m, after less than an hour of sleep, Roy's eyes snapped open. In one minute he changed into a sweatsuit and sneakers, put another change of clothes in a small bag, and ran off. He jogged through town, in no direction in particular, simply running loops around residential and business streets until the sun appeared over the horizon. Then he made his way to the address, a small tenement property of one-room self-contained apartments, occupied mostly by students from the nearby Federal University.

He got there drenched in sweat. But even though he'd been running nonstop for more than twenty miles, his breathing was still steady. He went to Ahmad's room and the door was pulled open before he knocked.

It looked like Ahmad had just got back from his own run. He had showered off the sweat, but somehow Roy could still feel his elevated heart rate.

"Can I use your bathroom?" Roy said, and was pointed in the direction. After a cold shower, he changed clothes and returned to the bedroom cum living room.

Ahmad's laptop was running on the bed. The screen was split into three live feeds of three other teams of agents and handlers. Roy said his greetings, made some small talk with the other field agents -- his own peers -- before they got down to business.

"Four of us," Ahmad explained, "are in charge of working the North Central states. They've all been briefed about your idea. And everyone agrees it's worth a try. So now you're going to be running pointer on the op. How do you want this to go down?"

Roy wasn't a bit flustered by the new attention and responsibility. He said, "It's simple. We just pick a joint. The less avenues for escape, the better. You guys -- Control -- spook them by setting up fake police stings. But we won't be using real cops, obviously. In the panic they'll scatter. Meanwhile, us -- the ground troops -- would lie in ambush and grab the isolated target. Then we rendezvous at the safe house for questioning. The guy'll definitely give us a higher up source. We bring in that one, get his source. I'm betting that the second or third name we get will be the same across board."

He shrugged to signify that he was finished. He looked around expectantly for questions. There were none. But he could still feel a small vibe of apprehension from his audience. Not because the plan had any holes, but because it seemed too easy.

He smiled. "Look, guys," he said. "Even if by the shittiest stroke of fortune this doesn't work out, there's still two dozen other teams who'll be doing it the regular way. This is definitely worth a shot."

He could see their doubts give way to the logic.

"Alright then," a handler said. "When do we move?"

"Twenty hundred."

* * *

Twenty hundred was military speak for 8 p.m. Half an hour before, Roy and Ahmad were ready to go. Ahmad had just returned from a police station where he showed his NIC badge and ordered that he would need a unit for a sting the following morning.

It was actually a ploy to give the pushers false security, since the news would definitely get to them through the cops on their payroll. The NIC used military officers for their less clandestine operations.

At ten minutes to eight, Ahmad lugged a large briefcase onto the bed and opened it. Roy smiled at the contents. There were various field equipment including guns, tasers, grappling hooks, and body armor.

Roy took a nylon cord and a set of nightvision goggles, along with a field communication transceiver the one in his briefcase back home. It was like miniature walkie talkie with nearly unlimited range. Ahmad took one field comm, and added a gun. Roy wouldn't need one. His hands were better weapons.

The joint they chose was a secluded area behind a community market. Three paths connected it to the outside world. Two to the open street, and a narrow fifty meter alley leading to the market, which was still bustling with activity.

After a quick recon, Roy positioned himself halfway down the alley, and waited. He didn't wear the goggles yet, so the dim green glow of the lens wouldn't give him away. He put a finger to his ear and told Ahmad he was in position.

"Roger," Ahmad said. "Moving in now."

Roy breathed slowly, enjoying the adrenaline rushing through him in anticipation of the coming battle. He

knew his target, and from his recon
he knew that there were eight other
people smoking there with him. They
would all come running down the alley
at Ahmad's prompt in less than a
minute.

Roy smiled. It was his first taste of
field action.

It happened without warning.

A series of deafening gunshots
stunned everybody, followed by Ahmad
shouting, "POLICE! ALL OF YOU LIE
DOWN!"

Roy strapped on the goggles. A few
seconds later a stampede of nine
terrified men surged down the alley
toward him. He could see every one of
them clearly. Nine against one.

Too bad, he thought. They should have
brought more men.

He floored the first one with a solid
kick to the chest that crushed his
sternum. Before that body dropped, he
whirled around and drove an elbow

into another solar plexus. The third one received a knee to the face.

All three bodies fell almost at the same time, and the other six stopped in confusion. Their hesitation was their undoing. Roy dropped them all with rigid chops to the neck.

It took less than ten seconds. Roy secured the pusher's hand with the nylon cord just as Ahmad jogged to the scene.

"Shit," he said, surveying the damage Roy had done. "Remind me never to get on your bad side."

Roy laughed, and together they bundled the target into the trunk of their car. Then they left, leaving no trace of their presence here, save the eight unconscious bodies in the alley.

* * *

The pusher was startled awake with a splash of water on his face. He looked around like a frightened rabbit, and immediately felt a needle jab into his arm. He stared at his captors, a young man and a boy half his age. Confusion was clear on his face.

"Who the hell are you people?" he said in a guttural yoruba. "Do you know who I --" he stopped, feeling a strange tingle in his system as the drug he was injected with started to take effect. He soon had a comical grin on his face.

Ahmad had injected the pusher with a brand of synthesized heroin manufactured by the agency for interrogations. Unlike what was portrayed in movies, physical pain was a terribly unreliable way to get information. The prisoner would tell you whatever you wanted to hear to stop the pain, and valuable time could be wasted separating fact from fiction.

This drug acted like a truth serum, making the subject so agreeable they'd confess everything to you.

Ahmad and Roy stood over the giggling drug pusher who was strapped to a chair. Roy was holding the pusher's phone, which they'd retrieved from his unconscious body. He was going to be asking the questions.

Roy stepped forward.

"My guy, my guy," the pusher said. "What's going on now."

Roy didn't waste any time on preambles. "Who's your supplier?" he asked in yoruba.

"Ha ahn," the pusher said and laughed, as if it was the silliest thing he ever heard. "You don't know Crusher?" he cried. "He's the boss now."

Roy checked the phone's contacts. He couldn't help but smile. These guys made it so easy. He found the Crusher name without sweat, and there were even several incriminating messages of their dealings on full display. He showed it to Ahmad.

"One down," Ahmad said. "Let's go get this guy."

He fed the number into a computer program that used a mixture of satellite imaging and cell networks to pinpoint the location of a phone to the last square inch of land.

Due to the powerful satellite, the process took only a couple of minutes. Crusher was in a bar at the moment, but from his phone's recorded activity, they were able to deduce the location of his house. Ahmad decided to head out there for recon, while Roy watched the prisoner.

Roy put the pusher to sleep by jabbing a cluster of nerves on his temple, then settled down to wait, playing a video game on his phone to pass the time.

Ahmad returned less than an hour later. He described the house as a middle-class tenement apartment. There were no armed guards or any other causes for concern, so they were free to move in as soon as Crusher was home.

That happened three hours later, shortly after midnight. From the lessons at the camp, Roy learnt that the best time to lay siege on a residential building was between three and four in the morning, when the occupants would still be in the deepest throes of sleep. So they agreed to move in at half past three.

"Try and get some sleep," Roy said.

Ahmad didn't argue. *Sleep when you can* was an age-old army rule. He knew that Roy could function at hundred percent without sleep for another two days.

He woke up at three o'clock sharp, and they got ready. Unlike the first round, this time they put on tactical harnesses and armed themselves with flashbangs and anaesthetic dart guns, as well as nightvision goggles. At half past three they were gone.

The property was fenced, but they scaled silently over the nine foot wall like cats. They made no sound as they went to Crusher's apartment. The entire compound, as well as everywhere else was silent. It seemed like they were the only living things

in that area, which suited their
purpose well.

Ahmad picked the front door's lock,
and they crept inside. The house had
two rooms. Crusher was asleep in the
first room they checked, with what
they guessed was his wife beside him.
Both man and wife were given a dart
each to make sure none of them
stirred as the secret agents secured
Crusher and took him out of his
house.

Ahmad went over the wall first. Then
Roy pushed over the sleeping man
before joining them on the other
side. And just like that, they were
gone.

* * *

Unlike the first pusher, who had been
knocked unconscious using physical
means, the agents had to wait for the
dart's chemicals to wear out of
Crusher's system. But after that,
when he woke up six hours later, he
was given the truth serum and

willingly gave the name and number of his own source.

That name was two levels above the streets, and if Roy was right they should start getting matches with the other groups.

And he was. Two of the three other teams had the same name and number. It was a retired Civil Defence commissioner who was now based in Abuja.

Mission accomplished. And in less than two days. Had they pressed with the original plan, they wouldn't have done anything for another five days.

They relayed this information to all the other teams across the country. Ahmad, meanwhile went to Abuja to join in the capture of the ex-commissioner. And Roy was sent home with a pat on the back.

Not that he needed more. The feeling of actually making a difference was enough. Plus, he had a laptop, a phone, and agency funds to plunder.

He heard nothing from Ahmad for another week. By then his dad had returned, and things were seemingly back to normal, though every morning at three Roy snuck out for his run, and didn't return until noon, after exhausting himself -- or trying to -- in a gym.

Then one night all the news media outlets in the country carried a spectacular headline…

NIC STRIKES AGAIN : SIXTY-THREE PAST AND PRESENT GOVERNMENT OFFICIALS ARRESTED ON CHARGES OF DRUG TRAFFICKING.

Roy was playing FIFA when he saw the news. Of course the public broadcast didn't carry his part in the operation. Then he received a message from Ahmad.

"Good job," it said. "One more mission accomplished."

Roy put his phone away with a smile. And resumed his FIFA game on the laptop.